Love

Grandma : Papa

This book is dedicated to my grandchildren

Lyric, Fields, and Cruz

Raymond and Archie

Eliza and Arden

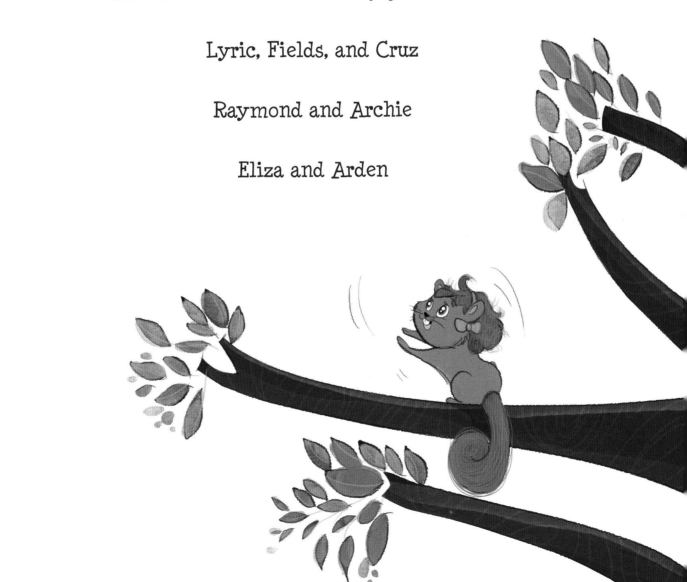

www.mascotbooks.com

Be Brave, Archie!

©2020 Linda Bergman Floersch. All Rights Reserved. No part of this publication may be reproduced, stored in a retrieval system or transmitted in any form by any means electronic, mechanical, or photocopying, recording or otherwise without the permission of the author.

For more information, please contact:
Mascot Books
620 Herndon Parkway, Suite 320
Herndon, VA 20170
info@mascotbooks.com

Library of Congress Control Number: 2020900681

CPSIA Code: PRT0620A
ISBN-13: 978-1-64307-538-9

Printed in the United States

LINDA BERGMAN FLOERSCH

Illustrated by Vanessa Alexandre

BE BRAVE, ARCHIE!

Archie and Eliza were both the same age and were first cousins. Their mommies were sisters. Archie had a big brother and Eliza had a little brother. They were all cousins. Archie and Eliza **loved** playing together.

They liked to play hide and seek.

One fall day, after all the leaves had fallen off of the trees, the cousins decided to go play in the huge old trees at the park.

Archie was excited so he took off running down the sidewalk.

"Stop, Archie, stop!" yelled Eliza. Archie heard Eliza but just chuckled and ran faster. He wanted to beat Eliza to the park.

Eliza **raced** to grab Archie's tail,
stopping him in his tracks!!

Just then, a big red trash truck

ZOOMED

right in front of Archie!!!

"You know Archie," Eliza explained,

"You **never** just run out into the street! You **always** watch for cars!"

"You're right Eliza," Archie agreed, shaking out his tail. "I'll be more careful from now on. **Sooooo, can we go play now???**"

At the park, Eliza and Archie had fun running on the fall branches without all of the leaves hitting them in the face.

"Faster, Archie, faster," yelled Eliza as she raced from branch to branch.

Eliza ran so fast that when she came to the tip of a long branch, without even thinking about it, she jumped! **Weeeeee**, she shouted, as she flew through the air. **But**, where did she go??

"**Eliza!!!**" Archie yelled. "I can't believe you just jumped **way** over to that other tree!!! You could have fallen!!"

"Don't be silly, Archie, it's fun!
Come on, **you can do it!**"

Archie looked down at the ground.

"I can't do **that**---I **will** fall!"

"Just take a run at it, Archie," Eliza begged. "You **can** do it!"

But Archie was too afraid.

Eliza finally gave up and ran back to the tree that Archie was in.

"Archie," Eliza said softly. "It's okay."

"If I can do this, you can do this,"
Eliza said. "Watch me."

Eliza ran and made the jump again.

"See, Archie," Eliza yelled,
"It's easy! Try it!"

After seeing Eliza make another jump safely, Archie started to feel BRAVE.

Archie backed up - - - -

took a deep breath - - - -

and ran as **fast** as he could!

And there
he went!!

Bravely flying through the air with his tail waving behind him.

"Yay!!!" Archie shouted. "I made it!!!
Let's do it again!"

And the cousins did make the jump again and again.

When the sun was going down, the two cousins decided to go home. Watching for cars as they crossed the streets, Eliza and Archie talked all the way home about their fun day.

"Can we do this again tomorrow?" asked Archie.

"Sure we can," answered Eliza.

"See Archie, a new adventure can be fun."

THE END

ABOUT THE AUTHOR

Linda Bergman Floersch lives in the Kansas City area with her husband of fifty years. One day, Linda decided to be brave and write a children's book based on something she saw out her kitchen window years ago. She has three children and seven grandchildren, and she decided to use two of her grandchildren as inspiration for the characters in this book. Do you see the blue bird on each page? That's Linda, watching lovingly over Archie and Eliza.